Chuck
The Unlucky Duck

Written by Morgan Matthews
Illustrated by Paul Harvey

Troll Associates

Library of Congress Cataloging-in-Publication Data

Matthews, Morgan.
    Chuck, the unlucky duck.

    (Fiddlesticks)
    Summary: Chuck comes from a long line of very lucky
ducks, but he does not seem to share their good fortune
until his search for a good luck charm gives him a new
perspective on his luck.
    [1. Luck—Fiction. 2. Ducks—Fiction] I. Harvey,
Paul, 1926-   ill. II. Title. III. Series.
PZ7.M43425Ch   1989   [E]   88-1284
ISBN 0-8167-1333-2 (lib. bdg.)
ISBN 0-8167-1334-0 (pbk.)

10   9   8   7   6   5   4   3   2   1

Chuck Duck came from a family of very lucky ducks. Good things always seemed to happen to Chuck's relatives.

Chuck's Uncle Mallard was picked to be on a TV quiz show. He ended up winning the grand prize—a year's supply of birdseed.

Great-grandma Duck entered a cooking contest. Her recipe took top honors.

Cousin Woody Duck was lucky, too. He went into a department store to get out of the rain and won a prize for being the one-millionth customer. Woody won a free trip south during the winter.

Everybody in the Duck family was lucky—
except Chuck. Nothing ever seemed to go
right for him.

If he needed to get someplace fast, he got
stuck in traffic and was late. If a package
was marked *Fragile,* he managed to drop it.
If he planted his vegetable garden in early
spring, it snowed the very next day.

All sorts of things always went wrong for
Chuck. "I'm jinxed," said the little duck
sadly. "Bad luck just seems to find me."

Because he thought he was jinxed, Chuck didn't like to be around his lucky relatives.

When he was invited to Uncle Mallard's birthday party, he wanted to stay home. But Uncle Mallard was Chuck's favorite relative. So, finally, Chuck went to the party.

"So far, so good," said Chuck, as he closed the door to his car and walked toward the house. "Nothing unlucky has happened yet."

Chuck stopped near the front door and reached for the knob. Suddenly, the door flew open.

Whack!

"Ouch!" yelled Chuck. "My beak! You bruised my beak!"

Out stepped Cousin Woody. "Gee, I'm sorry, Chuck," Woody apologized. "I didn't see you there."

Chuck rubbed his sore beak. "It's okay," he answered. "It was just some bad luck. I'm used to it."

Together, Chuck and Woody went into Uncle Mallard's house.

Chuck saw his uncle near the refreshments. He reached into his pocket and took out a small gift. It was in a little box.

"Happy Birthday!" Chuck said, starting toward Uncle Mallard. But luck wasn't with Chuck. He tripped over a footstool.

"Whoops!" he yelled, as he fell. Down went the duck. Up into the air went Uncle Mallard's present.

8

Splash!

The gift landed right in the punch bowl.
Slowly, it sank to the bottom.

"Ah, thanks for the present," Uncle
Mallard said. "What is it, a submarine?"

Chuck sighed and fished the gift out of the
punch. "It's a watch," said Chuck, as he
handed it to Uncle Mallard.

"A watch!" cried Uncle Mallard, opening
the box. The soggy timepiece refused to tick.
"Is it waterproof?" he asked hopefully.

"You mean punch-proof," joked Woody,
as everyone laughed.

From that moment on, things got worse
for Chuck. At dinner, he dripped soup and
stained his favorite tie. When he danced with
Great-grandma Duck, she stepped on his
foot. When he sat down in the living room,
his chair broke and he fell on the floor.
It was one thing after another.

Finally, it was time to sing "Happy Birthday" to Uncle Mallard. Great-grandma carried in a giant birthday cake.

"That cake looks heavy," said Cousin Woody. "Let me help you."

Woody walked toward Great-grandma. He accidentally bumped into her.

"Look out!" she called, as the cake went flying.

"Duck!" yelled Woody. Uncle Mallard did duck. The cake sailed over his head. It hit Chuck right in the face.

Splat! Chuck was covered with cake. Icing oozed over his eyebrows and onto his bill.

Cousin Woody laughed and shook his head. "Chuck," he said, "when it comes to bad luck, you sure take the cake."

Chuck got cleaned up and decided to go home. He'd had enough for one night. Before he left, Uncle Mallard took him aside.

"Chuck, you need some good luck," Uncle Mallard said.

"I know," Chuck replied, "but how can I change my bad luck to good?"

Uncle Mallard scratched his head and thought. "Try a lucky charm," he suggested. "A four-leaf clover is lucky. A new penny or a horseshoe may bring you luck. Luckiest of all is a rabbit's foot."

"Right! A good-luck charm," said Chuck. "Thanks for the advice." He smiled at his uncle and went out the door.

Chuck got in his car and drove off into the night. The drive through the shadowy woods was peaceful and quiet.

Suddenly, Chuck heard a strange noise, and an unlucky one at that.

Pop! Hissss! Flop! Flop! Flop!

"Great," grumbled Chuck, as he pulled off the road. "This is a fine time to get a flat tire."

Mumbling and grumbling, Chuck got out and opened the trunk. As he bent over to look inside, he hit his head. *Bump!*

"Ooooh," he moaned. "What can go wrong next?"

What could go wrong next? The answer
was in the trunk. It was empty. There was
no spare tire.

"Oh no," said Chuck. "I'll have to walk
all the way home."

Chuck waddled along the dark road,
complaining every step of the way. "What
a miserable night! What a rotten party!
What a crummy thing to happen!"

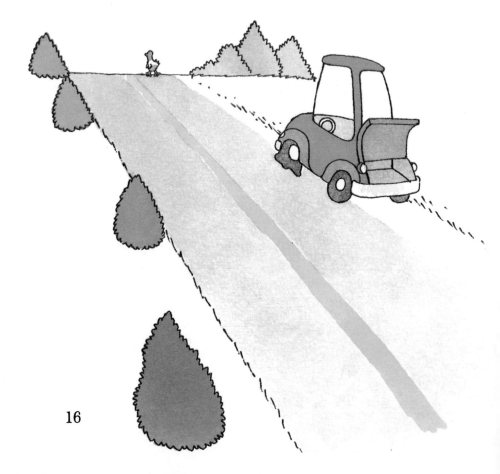

Hours later, Chuck finally reached his house. His flat feet were sore. His tail feathers were dragging. He was tired!

"I can't wait to get into bed," he said. He reached into his pocket for the keys.

"The keys!" he groaned, when he found his pocket empty. "I left them in the car. I'm locked out!"

Sadly, Chuck slumped down on the front
stoop. His eyelids began to close. Soon he was
snoring loudly.

The next morning he awoke with a bad
backache. As he struggled to his feet, a milk
truck pulled up. It was Marty Moose. Marty
and Chuck were good friends.

Marty walked up, carrying a quart of
milk. "What happened to you?" Marty asked.
"You look awful."

Chuck told Marty about the party, the flat
tire, and the long walk home. Being a good
friend, Marty offered to help. Marty drove
Chuck to his car to get the house keys. He
helped him fix the flat tire, too.

"Thanks for the help," Chuck said.
"Would you like to come inside for some
breakfast?"

Marty shook his head. "I have to finish my
milk route," he explained.

"Well, if there's ever anything I can do for
you," said Chuck, "just name it."

Marty's face brightened instantly. "Well,"
he answered, "there is something you could
do."

Marty took out a book of raffle tickets. "There's going to be a raffle," he explained. "I have a lot of tickets to sell. Would you buy one? It's for a good cause. And if your ticket is picked, you'll win a big prize."

"Sure," said Chuck. "I'll be happy to buy a ticket."

Chuck gave Marty the money for a ticket. Marty gave a raffle ticket to Chuck.

"Maybe you'll be lucky and win the prize," said Marty. "What number did you get?"

Chuck looked at his ticket and frowned. "I got number thirteen," he answered.

"Well, good luck anyway," said Marty. The moose got in his truck and drove away.

Chuck made himself some breakfast. As he ate, he thought about his bad luck. Then he remembered Uncle Mallard's suggestion. "A lucky charm," he said. "Maybe that *is* what I need." Chuck decided to find a good-luck charm that very day.

Around noon, Chuck left the house.
The sun was high and hot.

"It's a good day to go swimming," said
Chuck.

Chuck Duck liked to swim. In fact, he
was probably the best swimmer in the entire
Duck family. But he didn't have time for
swimming now. He needed to find a lucky
charm. The problem was . . . where?

Chuck didn't know where to look for a lucky charm. So he just started walking. Suddenly, he spied something round and shiny lying in the dirt.

"A penny!" he shouted. "My luck is changing already. Find a penny, pick it up, and all that day you'll have good luck!"

Eagerly, the little duck rushed over to the bright penny. It glittered in the hot sun. He bent over and picked it up.

"*Yeow!*" yelled Chuck. The sun had made the penny hot. "My fingers—I burned them," cried the duck, dropping the hot coin.

The next day Chuck tried again. He was
determined to change his luck.

"A four-leaf clover is good luck," he said.
"I'll go to the meadow and search for one."

The meadow was full of flowers and
clover. It was also full of busy, buzzing bees.

"Now to find a good-luck charm," said
Chuck, as he began his search. He looked and
looked without any luck. And as he did, he
bothered bee after bee. Soon the bees began
to get angry.

At long last, Chuck spotted what he was
hunting for. "A four-leaf clover!" he
exclaimed happily.

Chuck Duck plucked his lucky charm out
of the grass. "What great luck!" he said.
But was it really lucky?

It wasn't lucky for Chuck. The bees in the meadow began to swarm. They buzzed angrily. Then they began to sting.

"Ouch! Yeow! Ouch!" yelled Chuck. "Get away! Beat it, bugs!"

But the bees wouldn't stop. There was
only one way to escape them. Chuck ran for
the pond, clutching his unlucky good-luck
charm in his hand.

Splash!

Into the lake dove the little duck. When
he hit the water, he let go of the four-leaf
clover. Away it floated.

When the bees finally flew away, Chuck climbed out of the lake. "I won't give up," the wet duck said. "I've got to change my luck. Tomorrow I'll look for a horseshoe. Maybe a horseshoe will be lucky for me."

The next day Chuck started out to look for
a lucky horseshoe. As he neared the lake, he
heard shouting.

"Help! Please! Someone, help me!" said a
voice.

Chuck began to run. "Hang on," he
shouted. "I'm coming."

When Chuck reached the lake, he saw a big rabbit splashing wildly in the water.

"Help me!" screamed the rabbit. "I fell in! I can't swim!"

"I'll save you," shouted Chuck, as he dove into the water. Quickly, he swam to the rabbit. "Stay calm," Chuck told the bunny. Then Chuck grabbed the rabbit and towed him to shore.

"What happened to you?" asked Chuck.

"I had some bad luck," the rabbit said. "I slipped in the mud and fell into the lake. I couldn't get out."

Chuck stared at the rabbit in surprise. Uncle Mallard had said a rabbit's foot was the luckiest good-luck charm of all. And the bunny sure had big rabbit's feet. How could he be so unlucky?

"It was lucky that you came along when you did," the rabbit said to Chuck. "Thanks for saving me."

Chuck blushed. "It's lucky that I'm a good swimmer," said the duck.

The rabbit nodded. "You were sure *my* lucky duck. Thanks again!" And the rabbit hopped off down the path.

"Me? Lucky?" mumbled Chuck. "Lucky that *I* came along? That's what the rabbit said."

Chuck thought about what had happened. It was lucky that he'd gone to look for a horseshoe. It was lucky that he'd heard the rabbit's call.

Strangest of all, the rabbit who was supposed to be so lucky had been the one to have bad luck. It was all very puzzling.

"Maybe I'm not jinxed," said Chuck.
"Maybe there is no such thing as a lucky
rabbit's foot or an unlucky duck." The more
he thought about it, the more Chuck knew he
was right.

"Sometimes you have good luck," he said
as he skipped off happily. "And sometimes
you have bad luck. Right now I feel very
lucky."

When Chuck reached his house, he found
Marty Moose waiting for him. "Hi, Chuck!
You sure look happy," said Marty.

"I feel happy," answered Chuck. "And I
feel lucky, too."

"That's good," replied Marty.

"Why?" Chuck asked.

"Because today is your lucky day," Marty
explained. "I have great news."

Chuck Duck scratched his head in a puzzled way. "What news?" he asked.

"Remember that raffle ticket I sold you?" said Marty. Chuck nodded. "Well," continued Marty, "you won first prize!"

"*Hooray!*" shouted Chuck.

"What are you going to do with the prize money?" asked Marty.

Chuck thought for a minute. Suddenly, he knew exactly what he was going to do. "I'm going to throw a big party," Chuck answered. "I'll invite you, my relatives, and a rabbit friend of mine, too."

Everyone showed up the night of Chuck
Duck's big party. Marty Moose was there.
Uncle Mallard and Great-grandma Duck
were there. Mr. Rabbit was there, too.
The only one who was late for the party
was Cousin Woody.

"Congratulations on winning the raffle,"
Uncle Mallard said to Chuck. "You must
have found a lucky charm."

Chuck shook his head. "No. I don't believe
in lucky charms anymore," he told his uncle.
"I'm making my own luck from now on."

Up walked Great-grandma. "Is Cousin
Woody coming?" she asked.

Chuck smiled and nodded. "He should be
here soon. I'll go outside and take a look
around." Chuck went over to the front door.
He turned the knob and flung it open.
Whack!

"Ouch! My beak! The door hit my beak!" yelled Cousin Woody.

"Sorry, Cousin," apologized Chuck. "It was an accident."

"It's okay," said Woody.

"I'm glad you're here," Chuck went on. "You're just in time for the cake."

Mr. Rabbit and Marty walked out
carrying a big, beautiful cake. On the top of
the cake was written "GOOD LUCK,
CHUCK!"

"Can I see the cake?" asked Great-grandma. She accidentally bumped into Mr. Rabbit's elbow. He stumbled.

"Whoops!" yelled Mr. Rabbit.

"Look out!" shouted Marty, as the cake went sailing out of their hands.

"Duck, Chuck!" warned Woody when he saw the cake coming.

But Chuck didn't duck. He turned and caught the cake in midair.

"What a bit of luck," cried Uncle Mallard.

"What a lucky catch," said Great-grandma.

"Cousin Chuck," said Woody, "you really are one lucky duck." Everyone began to applaud.

Chuck smiled and bowed.

Splat!

He smacked his face right into the cake.

"Oh well," laughed Chuck, as he licked icing off his beak. "Sometimes you're lucky, and sometimes you're not!"